Maggi and Milo
Make New Friends

Juli Brenning

· illustrated by ·

Priscilla Burris

Dial Books for Young Readers

*To Mom and Dad for
everything, and to Ryan
for everything else.*
–J.B.

*To Jess, Lily, and Jason,
Chris and Christy!*
–P.B.

DIAL BOOKS FOR YOUNG READERS • *Penguin Young Readers Group*
An imprint of Penguin Random House, LLC • 375 Hudson Street, New York, New York 10014, U.S.A.

Text copyright © 2016 by Juli Brenning • Pictures copyright © 2016 by Priscilla Burris

Library of Congress Cataloging-in-Publication Data
Brenning, Juli.
Maggi and Milo Make New Friends / Juli Brenning; illustrated by Priscilla Burris.
pages cm • Summary: Maggi's mother persuades her to go to the park and make new friends, even though
her best friend, Milo, cannot join her because he is a dog. • ISBN 978-0-8037-3776-1 (hardcover)
[1. Best Friends—Fiction. 2. Friendship—Fiction. 3. Dogs—Fiction. 4. Play—Fiction.] I. Burris, Priscilla,
illustrator. II. Title. III. Title. PZ7.B75194Mam 2016 [Fic]—dc23 2015018793

Printed in China • 10 9 8 7 6 5 4 3 2 1
Designed by Jason Henry • Text set in Rough LT Com
The artwork for this book was created digitally.

Maggi and Milo

were having a staring contest.
Until . . .

"Maggi, let's go to the park," her mom said.
"Why?" asked Maggi.
"Because it's Tuesday and the sun is shining
and you might make a new friend," said Mom.

"The sun *is* shining and I *do* love
the park, but I don't need a new friend.
I have Milo—

the Mammal of All Mammals!"

"True, Milo is the Mammal of All Mammals," her mom said, "but it might be fun to play with a friend who can climb and talk and sing."

"Um," Maggi said.

She could climb and talk and sing herself, but Milo could do other stuff.

Still, Maggi and Milo ran straight for the playground.
Where there was a sign.

NO
DOGS
ALLOWED

"That is ABSURD!"
Maggi said. "Why
can't Milo come?"

"Because," said Mom, "the playground is for kids. Milo will be happy with me. You'll be fine on your own, Maggi."

NO DOGS ALLOWED

Maggi wasn't so sure.
But the kids did look like they were having fun, and *they* didn't have dogs.

"Milo, I'm going in."

"Hi. I'm Maggi," she said to a group of kids—one was wearing a tutu! "That's my dog, Milo. He's out there, and I'm in here. Can I play with you?"

"Sure," said the kid next to her. "My name is Antonio Carlos Enrique the third. You can call me Ace."

"I'm Sarah."

"And my name is Sydney, but I go by Amelia Earhart. We're playing hide-and-seek. You can hide, I will seek!"

"Actually," said Maggi, "I'm more of a seeker than a hider. Can you hide, and I seek?"

"Sure!" said Amelia Earhart.

They played hide-and-seek.
Then they played tag.

They climbed the jungle gym
and slid down the slide.

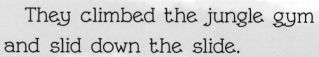

While they were swinging, Maggi sang a swinging song to her new friends.

(Of course, she did.)

It was fun. Really fun! The only thing that would have made it *more* fun was Milo.

"I think I will take Milo for a walk. He looks bored," Maggi told her new friends.
"Can we walk him, too?" asked Ace.
"Yes, but it's expensive."
"Expensive? Why?"

"Because Milo is the Hercules of Dogs and being the Hercules of Dogs comes with a big price tag. You understand, don't you?" said Maggi.

"Sure, how much?" Ace asked.

Maggi thought about an appropriate price.

"You may walk Milo for:

A family of roly-polies—
doesn't have to be a big family,
a small one will do.

3 white dandelions with their
cottony hair still attached....

5 yellow dandelions.

3 sparkly rocks—
the kind that look like diamonds.

I love those!

12 sticks of different lengths....

7 acorns—with their hats on, please.
Acorns like to cover their bald.

And 10 three-leaf clovers."

"Don't you mean four-leaf clovers?" asked Sarah.

"No, I mean three-leaf clovers, which are just as special as four-leaf clovers. They just don't get the respect they deserve," explained Maggi.

"We should split up," said Amelia Earhart.

"Ace, you find the roly-poly family, the sticks, and the acorns. Sarah, you are in charge of the dandelions and the three-leaf clovers. And because I am an expert on things that sparkle, I will find the diamond rocks."

(Apparently, Amelia Earhart had appointed herself spokesperson.)

"Okay," agreed Sarah and Ace, who were terribly agreeable people.

Off they went!

Maggi and Milo watched. Her new friends were having fun. Without her. Um. This wasn't working out as planned.

"Milo, I think I better help Ace. He looks like he could use a hand. Do you mind?"

Milo didn't mind.

If he could talk he would have told her that he loved watching her play with her new friends.

(But, of course, he can't talk. He's a dog.)

Under an enormous rock, Maggi and Ace found 1,004 roly-polies.
Sarah picked dandelions—yellow and white.

Amelia Earhart WAS a sparkle expert!
Once they had collected the payment, Maggi proclaimed,

"You may now walk
the Mammal of
of All Mammals,
the Hercules of Dogs,

Milo the
MAGNIFICENT!"

Amelia Earhart went first,

then Ace,

and then Sarah.

While each took a turn, Maggi played with the others.

Ace showed Sarah and Maggi how to make a pirate ship out of the sticks.

The acorns were the pirates, and the sparkly rocks were their booty.

Sarah showed Maggi and Amelia Earhart how to make a bracelet out of three-leaf clovers.

With the dandelions, Amelia Earhart, Ace, and Maggi made a house for the roly-poly family.

Then WAY before Maggi was ready to leave,
her mom called, "It's time to go home, Maggi!"
"One more minute?" Maggi pleaded.
"Half a minute, sweet girl. This day is done."

So half a minute later, Maggi waved good-bye to her new friends and hugged her old (and best) friend.

As they walked home, Maggi sang a quiet, end-of-the-day kind of song.

And then she said, "Thank you, Mom, for taking me to the park on this sunny Tuesday and thank you, Milo, for being magnificent. I think I like making new friends.

"But don't worry, Milo, you're still my very BEST friend."

Milo gave her a giant slurpy lick!

"I wonder what we'll do tomorrow, Milo?"

If he could talk, he would have said, I'm sure Wednesday will be just as much fun as Tuesday.

And, of course,
Milo would be right.